Enslaved

Atlantic City's Most Wanted #3

Charity Parkerson

Punk & Sissy Publications

COPYRIGHT

—Warning: This book is intended for readers over the age of 18. Some of my books contain allusions to past abuse and trauma.

CONTENTS

INTRODUCTION

HE HATES COURT. AS much as Heath bothers to dislike anyone, that is. That doesn't explain the satisfaction Heath feels when he wins him in a bet.

Court is one of the most sought-after escorts in Atlantic City. He has no shame. Having grown up in elite circles, he can fit in anywhere his next sugar daddy wants to take him. Men get into bidding wars for him. That's exactly why he should've thought for there to be a clause

1

about not betting him away in his contract. He never would've agreed to be with a spoiled daddy's boy like Heath. Now he's stuck.

From their first meeting, it was hate at first sight. Heath doesn't usually bother that much with anyone, but Court insulted him. So as far as Heath is concerned, Court started it. Now Court belongs to him and Heath plans to make his life miserable. Unfortunately, he doesn't consider—for once—he might be the bad guy and love might be the winner in the end.

Enslaved is the third book in Charity Parkerson's Atlantic City's Most Wanted series. These are sexy and sometimes dark stories where the richest and most dangerous men in Atlantic City meet their match. These are best enjoyed when read in order.

Author Note

THIS SERIES HAS SOME dark themes. This one has past trauma, addiction, and dealers.

CHAPTER ONE

TRUTH BE TOLD, HEATH actually enjoyed black tie events. He loved the gossip and there was a lot of that. Everyone talked about everyone else in hushed whispers. Heath learned all about who was screwing the pool boy and other people's spouses. As the son of one of the largest oil stockholders in the U.S., Heath had spent his life rubbing elbows with the rich. He had learned to spot the difference between new money and old.

His father had taught him how to tell by a man's dress if he was on the edge of losing everything. If there was one thing the elite had to do above all else, it was keep up appearances. But that was expensive, and his father's eye for failure was good. He had passed that to Heath.

That was exactly why it fascinated Heath that Wayne Kipper would have Court Langley hanging on his arm tonight. Court was an escort, and not a cheap one. Heath had never bothered to notice the guy before they recently had a very insulting exchange at a nightclub. But watching Court tonight was fascinating, considering what Heath had heard about his prices. Wayne was a man on the edge. His software company was deep in debt and one bad day away from going belly up. New money. They always got carried away with the excess.

Despite whom Wayne brought with him for the evening, Heath maneuvered his way through the crowd until he slid into the spot next to Wayne. Heath smelled gossip. He had to know more.

Wayne glanced over and smiled. His predatory gaze said he spotted a possible connection. "Heath. It's a been awhile."

Heath pretended to be surprised. "Wayne. It has been. I didn't even know you were here tonight."

A loud snort came from Wayne's other side, drawing Wayne's attention. "Oh." He dragged Court into view. "Have you met my date, Court? Court, this is Heath Overton."

Heath nodded.

Court did too.

Wayne smiled like the idiot he obviously was. "Court." Wayne pulled a credit card from the inside pocket of his dress jacket. "Why don't you go buy us some drinks?" He glanced Heath's way. "Do you want anything?"

Heath fought a snicker. Court had already walked away. He loved that his presence got under Court's skin. Heath shook the glass he already held. "I'm good."

Wayne looked back to where Court had been. For a moment, he looked confused before focusing on Heath again. "Anyhow, have you heard any news lately?"

It was always the same question. People always expected Heath to drop hints on which companies they should invest in. A smidgeon of pity hit Heath when he noticed the frayed buttonholes around Wayne's mismatched cufflinks. "Actually, yes. I have a good feeling about Tread-long tires. Their stocks dipped to an all-time low yesterday, making it dirt cheap. But rumor is, after signing a major face in football to a commercial deal, they landed a billion-dollar deal with a car company. My guess is they're about to skyrocket. You know how it goes. Buy cheap and sell high. You might want to keep that to yourself, though. I'd hate for the price to start climbing before you even leave the building tonight."

Excitement danced in Wayne's eyes. "That's great. Thank you. Of course, I won't say a word."

There. Good deed done for his lifetime. Heath shrugged. The tip really wasn't that big of a deal. Wayne could make of it what he wanted. "It's no problem. So, what about you? What's the juicy gossip going around tonight?"

Wayne chuckled and leaned his way. "Everyone's saying Prince Noir will bring the tattooed giant he married, but I say it's doubtful. The guy's only shown once with Noir. Not only did he look miserable the entire time, but he also scowled all night, scaring the hell out of everyone. I know he's a millionaire, but I still can't believe Noir married him."

Heath listened and tried not to laugh. Noir and his brute of a husband, Lazarus, were his friends. That gave Heath some insight. Noir fully intended to bring Lazarus. "I disagree. I think Noir enjoys the shocked expressions of his peers. He'll show."

Wayne's eyes lit with something dangerous. "Care to make a wager?"

The clouds parted and everything became clear. That was exactly how Wayne had tanked a lucrative business. Gambling addiction. He saw it now. The guy was always at the tables when Heath showed for a hand. Still, Heath wasn't one to back down. "What's the terms?"

It was more than obvious that was the moment Wayne remembered he had nothing to levy. His gaze moved across the room, as if buying time to search his mind. He froze and then met Heath's stare again. "I bet my contract with Court."

Heath's first reaction was a resounding hell no, but then he spotted Court headed back their way. The same mixture of hatred and unwanted desire washed over him. The idea of Court having no choice but to cater to him was a lot more intriguing than he liked. "And if you win?"

Wayne made a dismissive gesture. "You can just match the hundred and fifty thousand dollars left on the last two months of Court's contract. That way, the bet is even." He said the words so easily, as if Court nor the money meant anything.

Truthfully, a hundred and fifty thousand was nothing to Heath. He was oddly impressed Court got paid seventy-five thousand a month, but it was still nothing. Nevertheless, he pretended to chew over it, as if he wasn't that interested. Finally, he gave a sharp nod. "Deal." They shook hands.

Court appeared at Wayne's side with two glasses and the guy's credit card. "What did I miss?"

"Prince Noir and Prince Consort Lazarus Antonsen."

At the announcement of Noir's arrival, an evil grin slowly spread across Heath's face. Wayne let out a curse under his breath. Court looked between them, openly confused.

Heath focused on him, savoring the moment. He stared into dark blue eyes with a thrill he hadn't felt in ages. "It seems you belong to me now." It was every bit as satisfying as Heath had hoped.

If Court wasn't such a consummate actor, he might have dropped his drink at Heath's smug announcement. He looked Wayne's way. The shame written in his every line said it all. These men believed their words to be true.

"I don't know what you two are talking about, but it doesn't work that way. We have a contract for a reason." Normally, Court would never discuss the business side of things in public, but this was different. Any embarrassment Wayne felt, he had brought on himself.

Wayne nodded. He still didn't look Court's way. "We do, and I'm signing away the last two months of it to Heath."

Anger roiled through Court. He despised Heath, but it wasn't even that. Court wasn't a whore, nor was he cattle. No one got to choose to sell him. He chose his clients. "And again, it doesn't work like that. My contracts are a mutual agreement. I didn't agree to this." He made sure to focus on Heath, so the guy knew he wasn't wanted.

Oddly, he didn't look as arrogant as Court would have thought. "I'll have my attorney take a look at things tomorrow, since I know nothing about the specifics of your contract. If everything is in order, and it turns out this deal is good, then we can negotiate you breaking it. If not." He looked Wayne's way. His tone didn't change, but his gray eyes looked hard and unforgiving. Court wasn't looking at the carefree daddy's boy he knew Heath to be. "I'll expect a deposit of one hundred fifty thousand dollars in my account by the end of day Monday."

Court's gaze bounced to Wayne.

Wayne didn't look concerned. "The deal is good. I pulled myself up from nothing, Heath. I've never signed a contract in my life without reading every single word and understanding every loophole. This'll stand."

Court's stomach sank a little lower by the second. How had this happened? Fuck this noise.

Court squared his shoulders and shoved his drink Wayne's way, splashing it onto his clothes. "Since there seem to be a lot of different opinions here, I'll just go. You two can duke it out." He focused on Heath. The rage he felt bled into words. "And for the record, I'm not just some whore to be passed around. I am a legitimate and *legal* business. If that's not clear enough for you, I don't have sex for money. So you can wipe whatever smug thoughts are going through your head off your brain because I'm not the one." Court walked away before things came to blows. He would be damned if his professional appearance was damaged by this absolute bullshit. Court had known better than to sign with Wayne for three months. That was much longer than he usually gave anyone exclusively.

In fact, he had heard rumors of Wayne's business going under. Court had half expected the guy's check to bounce. Otherwise, he had seemed nice enough. The month they had spent together wasn't so bad. Wayne either understood sex was off the table or had been biding his time, because he hadn't once pushed. Court had been looking forward to a fairly quiet few months. Now he would have to pay a goddamn attorney to protect him from Heath. Heath. Fucking Heath Overton, of all people. Why did he even want Court?

Court collided with someone on his way out the door. Strong hands reached out to steady him. Court focused on a set of sweet and familiar light blue eyes.

"Court. Hey. Is everything okay?"

He almost cried at the sight of Portland. He was a longtime customer. Court also considered him a friend. He opened his mouth to say whatever it took to get out of there as quickly as possible. "No. Not really." His mind cleared a hair. He didn't have a way home. Since Wayne had driven, Court would have to find a cab. Fuck. He just wanted out.

Portland scanned the room, as if looking for someone before focusing on Court again. "Do you want to get out of here?"

Court nearly dropped to the floor in relief. "Please?"

With a nod, Portland had him by the arm and through the door in no time. He handed the valet his ticket before focusing on Court again. "We'll probably be waiting a minute. Tell me what's going on."

Court scrubbed at his forehead. He had never felt more humiliated. That wasn't true, but still. He hated this. Court just blurted it out. "Wayne sold me to Heath Overton."

Portland's eyebrows shot up. "He sold you?"

Court made a helpless gesture. "I walked away for like half a minute to grab a drink, and the next thing I know, boom. Wayne says I belong to Heath."

"There's no way that's legal."

The incredulous note to Portland's voice eased Court's shoulders a hair. He made a helpless gesture. "I don't know. Obviously, this isn't a situation I thought I'd ever find myself in, so who knows? I'm not a lawyer."

Portland's features cleared. He waved away Court's concerns. "There's nothing that can't be undone. If push comes to shove, I'll simply buy out the remainder of your contract."

While the air lightened some, the guilt was heavy, though. "I can't ask that of you. With Wayne, I intentionally set my price higher, hoping he would decline. It's a lot."

"How much is a lot?"

Court winced. "A hundred and fifty thousand for the remaining two months."

Not a muscle in Portland's face twitched. "That's nothing. I've got you."

Court wanted to cry. Only someone born to wealth would think that much money was nothing. While Portland worked hard to become the CEO of the largest bank on the east coast, it was an expensive education paid for by a disgustingly rich family that got him there. That made it twice as hard for Court's pride to admit the truth.

"Please don't. I can't afford to pay you back."

Portland closed the distance between them and set his hands on Court's shoulders. He was older than Court and better in every way. His salt and pepper hair looked purposefully done. Money did that. "If it comes to me paying your way out of this, then you can just be with me for two months. We always have a good time, and I don't care what people think."

Court knew that. That was why he had stopped charging Portland a long time ago. If he was free for the night and Portland needed him, Court was there. "Thank you for this. You have no idea how badly I don't want to be stuck with Heath."

Portland laughed as his Phantom rolled to a stop beside them. "Now that, I don't understand. He's quite the catch, but I can see you're serious." He led Court to the passenger seat as the valet opened the door for him. Portland helped him inside. "And I fully expect you to tell me why you're so against him as soon as we're on the road."

The valet closed the door, and Court fought a groan. He never wanted to talk about Heath and the night that obviously didn't happen between them.

CHAPTER TWO

THE DOORBELL RANG REPEATEDLY, dragging Court from the couch. He had only been awake for an hour and hadn't even had his coffee yet. His mind had been too busy. Court didn't know why he wasn't surprised to see Heath's stupid smiling face on his stoop, but deep down, he had known Heath would show.

"Good morning. I assume you heard from the attorneys." He stepped inside without being invited.

Court closed the door. Unfortunately, he had heard from his lawyer first thing. The contract was solid. There was no wording that stated it couldn't be sold. "Yes. I heard. Thankfully, Portland Wales intends to take on my contract, so..." As the words left Court's mouth, he realized the stupidity of them. If Heath had bought him from Wayne, then he likely wasn't interested in selling.

"No, thank you. I won you fair and square. Now—"

"Won me?" Court was too shocked to formulate a single thought.

Heath didn't give him time to rage. He gestured wildly. "I see the cogs turning in your head. Don't even think about it. There's also nothing in the contract that states you can't be wagered away."

Court couldn't decide which was more insulting, being sold or lost on a bet. Either way, Wayne was definitely on his blacklist now. "If you won't sell, then I'll just break the deal."

Heath shrugged and headed back to the door. "Fine. I'll see you in court and your reputation will be in tatters, but it's completely your choice if you want to ruin your business."

A growl rose and stuck in his throat. No one could possibly understand how much he loathed every second of this. "Fine. What are we doing today?"

Heath turned, all shit-eating smiles. "Excellent. Put on some shorts and grab your tennis gear. I have a court reserved."

For a moment, all Court could do was stare. Heath was for real, and it was a nightmare. "I don't play tennis."

Heath's smile somehow grew. "Well, then. Today is a good day to learn."

Court turned away. He could be the professional.

"Don't forget the comfortable tennis shoes."

The way Court wanted to start throwing punches was real, but he could survive two months. He had survived worse.

It was possible Heath didn't have to lob balls past Court at such a high rate of speed. He was actually a pretty good tennis coach. But Court still treated him like a burden rather than a client and—quite honestly—Heath had never wanted to break anyone as badly as he did the smug bastard across the net from him.

Heath threw up his hands when Court let another ball go flying past him. "Damn, Court. I know you said you've never played before, but I still expected better. You're not even trying."

Court stared at him with murder in his eyes. "I can't help it. You didn't listen when I said I don't know this game."

Heath made a dismissive motion. "Don't worry. You'll do much better at golf. I have a six-a.m. tee time scheduled for us so we can beat the heat."

The intent to kill didn't lessen in Court's expression. "I don't play golf either."

"Really?" Heath's surprise was genuine. He thought everyone in their circles played. "No golf. No tennis. Basketball? Squash? Croquet?"

"Nope."

Heath's confusion grew. "You're in great shape. What do you do? Don't tell me you just go to the gym and pick up weights. That's incredibly boring."

"As a matter of fact, that's exactly what I do." A wicked-looking smile stretched his lips. "Would you like to join me for that?"

Heath was fairly certain that smile was Court picturing his death. He waved his racquet. "Serve the ball the way I showed you."

While looking resigned as hell, Court retrieved the ball and did a somewhat decent job of serving. Heath swatted it back to Court. The ball hit him in the chest. The people on the court next to them laughed.

Court growled. "Why are you doing this? I don't understand why you have this perverse desire to always humiliate me. Tell me. Why?"

His explosion of anger was disproportionate to the day they had shared so far. But if Court was already ready to throw in the towel and have this out, Heath was game. The contract meant nothing to him. He didn't give a damn if he ever saw Court again. "I will as soon as you explain why you're always such a douche. You don't even know me. Yet the first time we met, you couldn't wait to toss insults my way." Even Heath couldn't explain why Court's jab about him being spoiled had stung so much. He was spoiled and didn't give a fuck. But—for whatever reason—coming from Court, it pissed him off.

"Don't know you," Court repeated, as if more for himself. His expression turned incredulous as hell. "Don't know you. I absolutely know you, Heath Overton."

Heath's brow furrowed at the hatred that dripped from Court's lips. "I never met you before the night Lazarus carried Noir from the club."

Court's expression snapped closed. His eyes turned dead. "Sophomore year. Five minutes in the closet."

"What the—" A memory creeped in. He had been at a party. There had been tons of drinking and a more risqué version of spin the bottle they had dubbed five minutes in the closet. He had spun the bottle and ended up with a chubby kid that didn't run in his crowd. They had five uninterrupted minutes in the closet to do anything. Back then, Heath hadn't been the least bit picky about who sucked his dick. Still, Court was full of shit. "That wasn't you."

Court simply stared at him, as if waiting for Heath to come to terms with reality.

Heath struggled to combine the vague memory of that night with the man standing in front of him. It didn't happen. "That wasn't you. If you went to school with me, I'd at least recall your name."

"Be real, Heath. You didn't know anyone outside your popular kid clique."

The confusion had him completely off guard. "It was just a stupid game."

"Was it?" Court sounded unbelievably cold. "I thought so too until you tumbled from that closet and told all your little buddies what a good little cocksucker I was." Court did the air quotes and everything.

The first hint of guilt hit. He might have done that. Everyone was a shithead when they were young and dumb.

Unfortunately, Court didn't stop there. "Do you have any idea what that did to my life? I got bullied and sexually harassed. Assaulted. It got so bad, I had to go to a different school. Not that it mattered. They had heard the rumors there too. That little game ended with me in the hospital when I tried to kill myself."

"I don't remember." Heath didn't know why that was the only thing he could think to say.

Court shrugged. "The hammer never remembers the nail." He threw down his racquet. "You know what? Sic your lawyer on me and ruin my reputation. It won't be the first time." Court walked away, leaving Heath alone and stunned.

For a moment, Heath simply stood there, trying to figure out what had just happened. Thankfully, it didn't take him long to rally. He grabbed their gear and ran after Court. Heath caught him as he reached the parking lot. "I drove."

"I know," Court called over his shoulder, sounding exactly like he thought Heath was dumb. "Ubers exist."

Heath jumped into his path. He walked backward as he tried to calm Court. "Would it make you feel better if I returned the favor? You could tell everyone I give terrible head, have a small dick, and cried afterward."

Court tried stepping around him.

Heath stayed in his path while still herding him toward the car. "Would it make a difference if I told you I bragged to everyone because no one had ever made me blow so fast? I was embarrassed."

Court stopped. "You were embarrassed because a fat nobody you didn't want made you lose control."

Actually, no. Heath seriously hadn't cared about Court's weight or looks. He just wanted to get off. Heath didn't think it would be a good idea to say as much. "Look, you pick what we do tomorrow."

Court huffed. "I told you. I'm done. Sue me."

Heath held his stare. "You can choose anything."

With a huff, Court shuffled from foot to foot. "You don't know when to quit, do you?"

"Nope. Come on. I'll take you home and you can think of a proper way to punish me tomorrow."

Court rolled his eyes, but he let Heath open the door for him. Heath took it as a good sign. He didn't know how to fix what he had done or even why he considered doing so. All Heath knew was he felt guilty, which never happened to him. For that reason alone, he had to make this right. Court didn't say a word on the drive home. Heath was more than a little surprised when he didn't jump from the car and run for the door the second Heath stopped in his driveway.

For a moment, Court stared at nothing. Finally, he blew out a breath. "Keep the s ix-a.m. tee time. If, and I'm serious about this if. If you swear to teach me golf for real, no more bs, we can finish out the contract."

Court didn't sound happy about bending for him, but Heath would take it. He didn't like this feeling that sat on his chest. Heath needed time to work through this in his head. The image he had in his mind of that night didn't line up with the man sitting next to him. Heath had to think about this. Until then, Court couldn't go away. He had to see this through.

CHAPTER THREE

THIS TIME WHEN THE doorbell rang, Court knew better what to expect. He had lain awake half the night, calling himself a thousand versions of an idiot. That didn't stop him from opening the door to Heath. He looked like a golfer. Court couldn't explain that thought. Just everything about Heath screamed he was on his way to the golf course. Court tried to treat this like just another job.

"Good morning. You look ready to play."

"Always look the part." Heath said the words like repeating from a script. Court found it odd, but moved on.

He stepped out and pulled the door closed behind him. "Obviously, I don't have any clubs or anything."

Heath shrugged. "I'm teaching you, re-member? You don't need clubs."

Court was oddly nervous. He didn't know why. Court never got apprehensive any longer. This felt different. He forced him-self to keep pushing forward. "How was your night?"

Heath looked equally confused by Court—like he expected more raging to-day. "It went." He opened the passenger side door for Court. Heath didn't contin-ue until he was behind the wheel. "I had dinner with my parents."

Court didn't know what to say to that. He knew nothing about Heath's parents other than their status in the community because the elite were a community. They held themselves above all others and tried not to mix. Court was only on the fringes because everyone knew his father. His dad was the dentist for the stars. He was also a gambling addict on the verge of always losing everything without Court.

"What did you do with your night?"

It seemed they would stick to the small talk. "Ordered in and binge-watched a show I've been wanting to see. It was good."

"That sounds way better than my night." Heath said the words under his breath, but Court didn't miss them. He could let it pass, but Court wasn't that strong.

"Do you not get along with your parents?"

"We get along fine." For a moment, Heath left it at that. After a few seconds passed, he broke. "It's just tedious. Everything is about image. It's like we're not even a family. We're just sitting together, trying to look like the perfect family—like we're not even real. Does that make sense?"

Court didn't want to care about anything remotely related to Heath, but he did get it. "Everyone is fake in this town. If all the spas and cosmetic surgeons left, there'd be nothing here but a bunch of snaggle-toothed, acne ridden, flat ass, pretentious people with small boobs."

"Except for the men," Heath said, adding to Court's list. He was smiling.

"Yep. Except for the men."

Heath's smile slipped away. He cleared his throat. His eyes stayed locked on the road while his grip visibly tightened on the steering wheel. "Um. Look. About yesterday, and every day, I suppose, I'm sorry."

It was definitely an apology Court never expected to get, especially since he truly believed Heath meant it. "I hope you're not expecting me to say you're forgiven."

A hint of a smile reappeared. "No. I don't expect anything."

The rest of the ride went by in silence. Court didn't know what churned through Heath's mind, but his jaw ticked—like he might snap at any moment. That fascinating tidbit had Court hanging back slightly, watching every minute detail of Heath interacting with people. Everyone they came across through the entire process of getting on the course got a different version of Heath. With older people—like friends of his parents—Heath was polite and reserved while being just the perfect amount of friendly. With the staff, he was all smiles. When they came across people similar in age to them, Heath brightened and said all the right things. Every single version of him was practiced and totally fake. Court was exhausted just watching it happen.

At the first hole, Heath transformed again. His features softened. He looked real. Court felt some way about that, but he didn't know what yet.

Heath handed him a club. "You need to stretch first." He showed Court how to twist from side to side, holding the club for support. "Okay. I have to touch you, but I swear it's completely professional."

Court spent a moment confused before Heath physically turned him toward the tee. The next thing he knew, he stared down at a ball with Heath's arms wrapped around him from behind. He helped Court align himself perfectly.

"You see the flag. What's it going to take to get there?" Heath's question brushed his ear. Court pulled his mind from that detail and tried envisioning the best way to hit that flag. "You got it?"

Court nodded.

"When I take a step back, I want you to take that image in your mind and combine it with exactly how much force you think you need to hit that ball to get it there."

Court nodded again.

Heath took a step back.

Court swung. The ball sailed through the air. He was actually kind of proud of how much air it got.

Heath watched it. "Not bad at all." He looked Court's way, smiling. "This might just be your game."

It was back. The flutter Court had felt all those years ago when he secretly lusted after the popular kid. Court looked at him now. That smiling boy everyone flocked to, and Court did everything in his power to get closer. It was him. What in the hell was he supposed to do with that?

By the eighteenth hole, the sun was relentless, beating down on them. Heath nearly sighed in relief when he spotted the cart girl headed their way. It didn't matter they were almost finished. He was dehydrated as hell. It was a state made worse by the continuous touching. He didn't want to be attracted to Court, but each time he corrected Court's stance, the desire got a little harder to ignore.

"Do you guys need anything to drink?"

Heath pasted on his friendliest smile. "Two waters."

"Sure thing."

While she dug two bottles of water from an ice chest on her cart, Heath pulled out a pre-folded bill from his pocket. It was perfectly tucked exactly as his father had taught him to keep anyone from seeing the amount. Only new money flashed their wealth. She handed him the waters. He discreetly passed her the bill.

She smiled. "Thank you, and good luck."

He handed a water to Court.

Court twisted off the cap. "You should let me tip sometimes."

The offer surprised Heath. Not only was Court contracted to be here, and should—therefore—have all expenses paid, but no one ever offered to pay with him. Heath automatically became his dad out of habit. "Old money always tips but never flashes their money."

Court eyed him for a second. "You really had some rules drilled into you as a kid, huh?"

Without his brain's permission, a smile exploded across Heath's face. "Old money wears brands so expensive no one has ever heard of them unless they have, but with no logos, of course. Those are your people."

Court's smile matched his. "Old money doesn't touch their car door or hand back a menu to a server."

"Ah. You've heard these."

Court shook his head. "I spend all my time with old money and I'm observant. It's a subtle difference between privileged and rude, but I see the fine line."

Heath scoffed. "I'd never be rude. No one wants to get labeled a diva."

They shared a smile.

Heath realized he was having a much better time than expected. "Have lunch with me."

To his shock, Court's smile didn't waver. "Okay."

It seemed crazy to press his luck, but he couldn't stop. All the way to the car, he plotted ways to keep making progress with Court. He had lain awake all night, thinking about the hurt and rage Court had flung his way. Heath didn't like it. While he might not be the nicest guy, he would like to think he wasn't the bastard Court believed him to be.

"I remembered something last night. When I said I would've at least known your name, I wasn't completely wrong. You didn't go by Court back then. You went by Andrew."

Thankfully, Court didn't look opposed to the topic. "Yeah. I used to get teased for Court, so I started going by my middle name."

Heath's forehead furrowed. "Why would you get teased over Court?"

Court shrugged. "Why does anyone get teased over anything? Kids are assholes."

He supposed that was true. "What made you decide to go back to Court?"

Court answered as they climbed into the car. "I stopped caring what anyone else thought. My mom named me after her childhood best friend. It was important to her, and I like the name, so fuck everyone else."

"Fair. Any lunch preferences?"

Court's phone chirped before he could respond. "Sorry. That's my front door camera alert." He pulled his phone from his pocket and clicked around. A low curse left his lips before Court pinched the spot between his eyes. "Sorry. I'll have to take a rain check for lunch. Do you mind taking me home?"

The immediate devastation on Court's face had Heath starting the car. "Not at all. Is everything okay?"

"Probably, but not likely," Court muttered before falling into a quiet stew.

Heath's nerves stretched from the strained quiet. His heart dropped when he pulled into Court's driveway. For some reason Heath didn't understand, Court's father, Drue, was doing his best to destroy Court's front door. It looked as if he had already demolished everything on the front porch. Heath didn't ask what was happening or if Court needed help. He simply parked and jumped out when Court did. Father or not, Heath wouldn't drive away and let Court get hurt.

"Dad. What in the fuck are you doing? You know you're not allowed here."

The guy's blond hair was a mess, and his clothes were wrinkled. He went from raving lunatic to perfectly calm at the sight of Court. "You moved your spare key."

Court scrubbed at his forehead. "You're not supposed to be here," he repeated, sounding tired. "I have a restraining order."

Heath was confused but invested. This was definitely gossip he hadn't heard.

Drue's dark blue eyes that looked so much like his son's moved between Court and Heath and back again. He looked more calculating by the second. "You weren't home, so I wasn't breaking the terms of the order. You're the one who showed up and is breaking it."

"You're at my house." The exasperation in Court's voice made Heath wonder how often this happened. "So, what? You just came to break in while I wasn't home?"

Drue shifted from foot to foot. "I didn't break in. The key is missing."

"You're the reason it's missing, Dad. I have nothing left to give you. Now leave before I call the cops. Mom shouldn't have to keep bailing you out."

Anger flashed in Drue's eyes. It was beyond obvious the pair had forgotten Heath stood there. "I'm your father. You wouldn't have anything without me." He jabbed himself in the chest. "I'm the one who worked his fingers to the bone so your spoiled ass could have the best of everything and look what it got me. Nothing but an ungrateful son who won't see his father."

"How much do you owe?" Court's voice sounded dead.

"It's not about that, Court."

"How much do you owe?" Court repeated.

Drue swallowed. "Seventy-five thousand."

"Sev—" Court paced away and ran his fingers through his hair, looking ready to tear it out by the roots. He turned back. "How did you even get that deep when you know you don't have it?"

Drue's hands rose and fell. "Saul knows I'm good for it."

"Saul... You're..." Court looked so enraged, almost like he didn't know where to start. "You're not good for shit!" He yelled the words at the top of his lungs. "You got in deep because you knew you could come crawling here. Well, you know what? Not this time."

Drue went from stoic to pleading in an instant. "We're talking about Saul Gabris.

I can't go back empty-handed to the god-damn mob. He'll kill me."

"Good." The spite in Court's voice nearly had Heath taking a step back.

"You don't mean that. No matter what, I'm still your dad."

Court sliced his hand through the air, as if he had heard enough. He dug his phone from his pocket. "You stopped being my dad when you chose your addiction over your family. I'm calling the police now. I seriously doubt Saul will kill you, since you have zero qualms about losing all my money in his casino. But maybe if he breaks your goddamn kneecaps, you'll learn your lesson, because I am fucking done."

The pleading turned to fury. The switch flipped so fast, Heath didn't see it coming. It seemed Court fully expected the attack.

"You ungrateful little bastard." Drue leapt from the porch steps, obviously prepared to jump Court, swinging.

Like he saw it coming before it happened, Court's fist shot out, landing in the center of Drue's face. Drue immediately hit the ground. Court stepped over him and headed for the door. Heath followed. He didn't know the full extent of what was happening, but he knew he couldn't leave Court alone.

Chapter Four

COURT HELD HIS PHONE in a death grip as he watched his dad from the window. He silently debated if he would actually call the police. It had taken him way too many years to find the strength to get a restraining order. He didn't know if he could keep taking things further. Court didn't want to lose his family, but seventy-five thousand? He couldn't even fathom losing that big.

"So your dad is a gambling addict?"

Court closed his eyes and wished for a meteor to take him out. The last thing he wanted was for Heath fucking Overton to play witness to his drama. "Yes."

"And you work as an escort to pay his debts."

It was obvious Heath simply tried to get a feel of the situation, but Court hated this. "In part, yes."

"Why does Saul continue to extend him lines of credit if he can't pay?"

Court waited until his father's car disappeared down the street before turning to face Heath. "Because his debts always get paid."

"By you?"

Court nodded.

Heath looked sympathetic. Court hated that, but Heath stayed. "Saul is a friend of mine. I'll quietly suggest he cut him off."

Court made a helpless gesture. "Will it matter? He'll just go somewhere else and owe someone else."

"It's better than doing nothing." Heath looked kind and understanding.

It was more than Court could take. His shoulders fell. He pinched the spot between his eyes again. Court couldn't think. He always felt so goddamn helpless. Heath's arms engulfed him. The kindness came from left field at his lowest point. Court couldn't pull away. He buried his face against Heath's chest and breathed. They had been in the sun, playing golf all morning, and he still smelled delicious. It was oddly soothing.

"So, look. I know I'm the last person you want with you right now, but I'm here. Go put on something comfortable, and I'll treat you to a relaxing day."

Court hid his smile. He didn't want Heath to know how his words eased the stress just by saying them. Court took a breath, rearranged his features into stoic, and took a step back. "Would you like to borrow something comfortable to wear?"

"I'm comfortable." Court stared at him until he was honest. "I'd love to borrow something."

With a nod, Court motioned toward the hall. "I'm sure I can find something." Together, they headed inside Court's bedroom. Court peeled off his shirt as he went and tossed it on the bed. He would throw it in the hamper later. With his back to Heath, Court dug through his dresser looking for shorts and a t-shirt for both of them. They were similar in size, so he wasn't worried. The one thing Court owned in droves was clothes. He found two pairs of workout shorts and two plain t-shirts. When he turned, he found Heath watching him. His face was completely clear of emotion, but his eyes burned.

Court's mouth went dry. He could not go back to the days of pleading with the universe for one shot. He passed the clothes Heath's way. "Here."

"Thanks." He looked around, as if searching for a place to change.

Court laughed as he stripped and pulled on the fresh clothes. "If you're shy, you can change in the bathroom."

As if Court had issued him a challenge, Heath set the clothes on the bed next to him and stripped. Court wanted to look away. God knew he did. There wasn't enough strength in the world. Inside, where no one could see, there was still a fat nobody who wanted this guy with the power of seven suns. There wasn't a force in existence that could tear his gaze from Heath.

"If you keep looking at me like that, I won't bother getting dressed."

Except for that. Heath, knowing Court wanted him, was enough to throw cold water on Court. He looked away. "The size of your ego is suffocating."

Heath smirked but didn't call bullshit.

Court tried to move on. "So, what do you want to do?"

For a moment, Heath simply stared at him, and Court knew exactly what he wanted to do. "Leave it to me. I'm an expert at relieving stress."

Holy shit. The way Heath said the words weakened his knees. Court knew he was in trouble, and he didn't know how to pull back. Before Court could think of a witty comeback, Heath gathered his clothes and patted the pockets of his pants until he found his phone. Having his attention elsewhere gave Court a second to breathe. They were sufficiently covered now, but Court still didn't feel safe standing so close to a bed. He headed for the door, hoping Heath would take the hint and follow him to the living room. With his head down and typing on his phone, Heath followed. Court tried not to think about anything. It had been a day. His dad's all too common outburst combined with spending the day with the guy who ruined his life should have had Court ready to break down. Instead, he practically held his breath, trying to anticipate what might happen next.

He sat on the couch, and Heath joined him. After a second, Heath's gaze lifted from his phone. "Okay. Surprise will be here in thirty. You want to make out until then?"

Despite everything, a smile exploded across his face. Heath was irritatingly irresistible. "Fuck. I hate you."

Heath's smile never dimmed. "That's okay. Hate fucking is supposedly a lot of fun."

Court laughed. He held his side. "Stop. You're ridiculous."

"Am I?" Heath turned so serious so fast, it killed the laughter in Court's throat. They held each other's stare. Heat bloomed between them. Court didn't want it.

He stood. "Can I get you something to drink? Maybe a beer?"

"Sounds good." Heath's smile looked fake again. That hurt Court's chest, but he still headed for the kitchen without looking back. For longer than he cared to admit, Court stood, holding open the refrigerator door while his mind drifted. He still felt the jolt of excitement mixed with terror as he had as that closet door had closed, leaving him alone with Heath. They hadn't made a sound. They had both known everyone listened on the other side. He swore their breathing got louder and faster even though they weren't touching. Then Heath's mouth had found his.

Court blinked. His mind shied away from the rest. He had lost the ability to relive this dream, turning into a nightmare a long time ago. But that sickness in his gut, that never went away. He wished for amnesia. Not because he wanted a second shot with Heath. He wanted a second shot at life. One where he entered the world with rose-colored glasses and full of hope. Bitterness welled in his chest. Except Heath wasn't the only bad memory. His father was just as guilty of ruining his life. Damn. He was tired. Court grabbed two beers and headed back to the living room. This was his life. He had no choice but to live it.

Throughout mani pedis coming to them and dinner and wine, all while cozy at home, Heath watched Court's mood go on a rollercoaster ride. Just the fact that he kept trying to pull himself from the funk said more than Court realized. He was strong.

With a movie playing in the background, Court was fast asleep. Heath watched him. The light from the TV was the only light in the room. The shadows danced across his face. Only because he knew now, Heath saw hints of the boy in that closet. It was funny. All the guys who laughed with Heath about that night had all disappeared from his life a long time ago. They were doctors or lawyers or no one at all. There wasn't a single one he could call for help, even back then. Maybe even especially back then. But Heath had a strange feeling he could call Court. Heath shook his head. Court looked uncomfortable with his head at a weird angle. He would wake up unable to turn his head if he stayed like that.

Heath glanced around. There was a blanket folded nearby and a couple of throw pillows on a decorative chair. Heath grabbed them and made the couch into a cozy bed. He eased Court onto his side, urging him in his half-awake state to lie on his side and spread out. Before he could stop himself, Heath joined him. He had been drinking and couldn't drive home. Heath knew he could call someone, but then his car would be here, and it would just be a pain. So, he covered them and snuggled in close. He was on the very edge of the couch, but he would keep Court from falling onto the floor.

It felt a little strange having Court in his arms. Heath tried not to breathe in his scent, but it was impossible. It didn't surprise Heath that men paid exorbitant amounts of money to spend time with Court. He was honestly... nice. That seemed such a simplified description, but he was. Court was kind. He had all the reasons in the world to hate Heath. Yet he had been kind today, as if he fully intended to give Heath a second chance. Heath didn't deserve it. He knew that. A good person would have walked away and given Court peace after learning they had ruined the guy's life the way Heath had. Heath was a lot more insecure than people realized. He couldn't stand being disliked. So much so, he wasn't even sure who he was anymore because he spent so much time being what everyone else expected. Things had felt different today. His shoulders weren't stiff. He had laughed for real. Heath couldn't leave yet. He didn't know why. He just couldn't.

A loud buzz had Heath searching for the source. Court's phone was on the coffee table, lit and moving. Heath grabbed it before it woke Court. He meant only to switch it to completely silent, but the texts spanning the face of his phone caught and held his attention. It was like a train wreck he couldn't look away from. Text after text rolled in, swapping between his mom and his dad, berating him for selfishness and blaming him for what might happen to his father. Heath's heart sank. He was exhausted by the snippets he caught. Heath couldn't imagine how Court felt. Without a qualm, he switched it to silent and hid it beneath the couch before going back to cuddling Court. Maybe one day of a missing phone would give him some peace. It was just a small thing, but Heath could work on the rest.

CHAPTER FIVE

THERE WAS NO CONFUSION. That was the scary part. Court woke up in Heath's arms with his face pressed against Heath's chest. He knew exactly where he was. Court didn't try to remedy the situation. In fact, he subtly snuggled closer. At least, he thought he did until Heath's arms tightened around him. That was when he realized Heath's arm was shoved beneath his shirt, skin on skin, as seeking warmth. From there, his mind cleared even more. Court had a majority of the couch while Heath hung on for dear life. Court also had the entirety of the blanket and the only throw pillow. Poor Heath was in the most uncomfortable, cramp-inducing position Court had ever seen. He smiled. Heath obviously had done everything possible to keep him comfortable and not wake him.

"I have some things to take care of this morning, but I'll be back this afternoon."

Court's smile grew. He didn't know how Heath knew he was awake. "I love how you assume I'm free today."

"Are you?"

"Yes."

The soft chuckle that rumbled from Heath's chest felt good caressing his ears. "Then I'll be back this afternoon."

Oddly, Court didn't want him to leave.

Heath made no move to get up, even though he had to be uncomfortable as hell.

Court was hyperaware of every place their bodies touched, which was basically everywhere, considering how they were squished together on the couch. Heath was hard, but it was likely morning wood, and he wasn't being disrespectful. It was nice to simply be held, even if it was only so Heath didn't fall off the couch. He searched his mind for a way to make the moment last a little longer.

"What do you want to do today?"

"Nothing."

Court laughed at Heath's answer. "But you're coming back today?"

"Yes."

He confused Court. "You want to do nothing together?"

"Yes."

Well, fuck. Court kind of wanted to punch him for turning out to be a nice guy. "Okay."

Heath still didn't move.

Court didn't either. Minutes ticked by. They silently cuddled. Court listened to the steady beat of Heath's heart.

"I really have to pee, but I'm too comfort-able to move."

A laugh burst from Court. "How in the hell are you comfortable in your position?"

He felt Heath shrug. "I'm holding you."

Oh no. He was in trouble. Everything felt too good. This would not end well for Court. Yet, he couldn't stop. "Run to the bathroom and come back. I won't move."

"We'd never get in this position again."

Court couldn't stop smiling. The entire situation was just so damn ridiculous. There was an intimacy that would break when they moved. Court couldn't stop himself from taking advantage before that happened. His fingers found their way beneath Heath's shirt. His lips found Heath's collarbone.

"Did you ask yourself how you could make this situation worse and then let the intrusive thoughts win?"

Court pushed him off the couch. "There, the demons won. Now you can go to the bathroom."

From the floor, Heath smiled up at him like an idiot. He was sleep-mussed and real. So fucking real. For the first time, Court knew he stared at the genuine version of Heath. He didn't know if he could survive him.

Heath rolled to his knees and jogged to the bathroom. He looked adorable. The most terrifying thought of all hit. He wanted more.

Heath made his way through the casino he knew like a second home. He wasn't a gambling addict like Drue or Wayne. Heath was just wealthy and bored. Plus, Saul was his friend. Saul ran several casinos in town. He was definitely the place to start. Heath had texted him before coming. That way, he wouldn't have to hunt for the guy.

Luckily, a person Heath recognized to be private security headed his way before he made it too deep into the place.

Heath nodded at the man. In a matter of minutes, Heath sat across from the man who helped run Atlantic City. He might've been terrified if he didn't know Saul so well. He had eyes so light, they cut through a person and a slight accent that intrigued people.

"Your message was pretty cryptic this morning. Is everything okay?"

Heath appreciated the genuine concern in Saul's voice. "Yes and no, I suppose. I'm perfectly fine. My friend, on the other hand, is not. You have a problem in Drue Langley. You need to stop his line of credit."

Saul's eyebrows rose. "Why is that? He's always paid his debts."

"No. He hasn't." Heath didn't hold back. "He's been shaking down his son for the money."

Saul sat back and sighed. "Honestly, I'd begun to worry. His losses have been suspiciously more than his salary should cover."

Heath nodded. "For Court's sake, I'll cover the seventy-five thousand he owes now, but from here on out, he doesn't have it."

Saul looked slightly confused. "He doesn't owe seventy-five. He only owes twenty."

Heath was every bit as confused. "Odd. When he tried kicking in his son's door yesterday, he screamed about seventy-five. Maybe he owes more than one casino?"

Saul shook his head. "Not possible. We all keep check. Only one high limit debt at a time. If you owe one, you won't be extended credit anywhere else." Saul paused. He looked as if he wasn't sure if he wanted to continue. Finally, he sighed and held Heath's stare. "There's a very real possibility it's not this addiction he can't pay."

Heath wanted to say he was surprised, but he wasn't. "Damn. When I saw the way he had destroyed Court's front porch and the insanity he showed, I thought that might be the case. Coke, I assume."

Saul dipped his chin. "Mac caught him snorting in the bathroom. He was thoroughly scared away from using my club for that bullshit."

Heath wouldn't touch that one. The huge guard, Mac, likely held the guy by his feet over a balcony. At least, that was what Heath pictured. "Do you know who his dealer is?"

"No. There's not many people it could be among the community, but it's not like you can go around asking."

Heath sighed. "Well, fuck. All I can do is cover his debt here and hope the other fifty-five was him wanting funds."

"May I ask why you're willing to do this? It's not like I don't have other ways to get the money from him."

A chill ran down Heath's spine. He didn't doubt Saul. "I'm not doing it for him."

For a moment, Saul studied him. His expression gave nothing away, but when he spoke, he sounded deadly. "Let me guess, he's the reason Court is selling himself."

Everything inside Heath revolted at the question. Court wasn't a whore. Logically, Heath knew people thought that because Court literally sold his time. But there was a part of Heath that felt like it was his fault. He had set Court on this path. Heath didn't like this feeling. Still, he knew what Saul meant. "I believe so, yes. Even though I don't know exactly how long Court has been bailing him out, I know he's done." Heath felt his face harden and his tone matched the change. "And Drue is a huge piece of shit who doesn't deserve the amazing son he's been given. I'll be damned if he continues to drag him down."

Saul's gaze moved over Heath's face. He nodded. "Court is lucky to have you."

A bark of laughter burst from Heath. "I promise he'd disagree."

A smile exploded across Saul's face. "We'll see."

It was scary how badly Heath hoped Saul was right. Heath wasn't looking for anything. He didn't expect his time with Court to go anywhere. But strangely, his morning with Court was the happiest he had been in a really long time. For that alone, he would spare Drue. Now he had to get back to Court.

Unfortunately, Heath didn't make it back to his car unmolested. Portland appeared from nowhere and blocked his path. A groan rang through Heath's head, but he kept his expression and tone bland. "Portland."

The guy's let's-do-business smile made an appearance. "Heath. I hear you've made a recent acquisition."

Heath swallowed his annoyance over everyone speaking about Court like he was an item at the store. "I need you to be more specific." He knew he was being a dick. Heath didn't care. Portland was just a little too shiny for him.

The congenial smile turned sharklike. "Court Langley."

"I know of him, yes."

Portland straightened his sleeves. "Perfect. I'd like to purchase his contract." Heath knew this game. His sudden focus on the press of his suit was meant to look as if the topic meant nothing to him.

"No." Heath stepped around him.

Portland jumped back into his path. "I'm quite serious. I'm willing to make you a very generous offer."

Heath squared his shoulders. "No." This time, he didn't walk away. He held Portland's stare, so the man understood he wouldn't be budged.

Confusion twisted Portland's features. "Why? It's obvious you can't stand him."

"Why do you want his contract? What would you do with it?"

Under his unwavering stare, Portland turned visibly uncomfortable. He shifted nervously. "I have no immediate plans."

Heath felt the way his intensity doubled. "The remainder of his contract is worth one hundred and fifty thousand dollars, and you just offered to pay even more. That's not the actions of a man with no plan. So, again, what do you plan to do with his contract?"

"I don't see why it would matter to you."

Heath didn't falter. "It matters."

Portland lost his shiny composure. "Why do want to keep him so badly? If you don't even like him and won the damn thing in a bet anyhow, why refuse to sell?"

Something dark rose inside Heath. It sounded in his voice. "This. For this fucking reason, right here. You're badgering me to buy Court like he's a goddamn object. He's a person. I might only hold his contract for the next sixty days, but for those months, he'll get to be the human fucking being he is. Now get the hell out of my way. I have places to be." While still fuming, Heath stepped around a visibly shocked Portland, leaving him behind. He considered going back and turning the argument physical while he waited for valet to bring his car. Heath couldn't count the number of times he had seen Court on Portland's arm and the guy still treated Court like he was nothing. Court was a person. This job was bullshit. Fuck everyone who had led Court into this position and trapped him there, including Heath. Heath was enraged, and he had no idea how to fix anything. All he knew was he wanted to get back to Court. So, that was what he would do.

CHAPTER SIX

COURT HATED WHEN HE couldn't remember where he left his phone. He had shaken down his clothes and searched all the usual places. Court didn't think he had left it in Heath's car, but he had jumped out pretty quickly at the sight of his dad melting down. It was possible. He had been distracted by Heath hiring a spa crew to come to them. Then Heath had fed him and found them something to watch. It hit Court. He remembered checking the time on his phone before setting it on the coffee table. Court searched around the table, going as far as to move it and check beneath. He had no idea how much jostling had gone on in the night for them to end up so entangled. Plus, Court had shoved Heath off the couch. It was likely Heath had hit the table. Court winced. He hadn't considered that before now. Court dropped to his knees and peered under the couch.

"Ha. There you are." Court dug his phone from beneath the edge of the couch. He had missed hundreds of texts. "Damn. I should've left you under there." With a sigh, Court plopped down on the couch and started scrolling. It was the usual spiral from both his parents. This time, though, Court wouldn't give in. He was really done this go around. Seventy-five thousand was the breaking point. That eye-popping number proved exactly how far his dad would go with no regard for Court, or anyone, for that matter. He couldn't do this anymore. Court barely skimmed the texts, feeling nothing any longer. They had beaten him down years ago. His scrolling slowed as he came closer to the end. The tone changed. Suddenly, he was being praised as the amazing son they knew him to be. Court paused to actually read. His dad's debt had been paid. The phone dropped to Court's lap. He stared at nothing. It didn't take much mental math to figure out how that debt had disappeared. Court didn't know how he felt. On one hand, this would only embolden his father to continue spiraling. On the other, why? Why would Heath do this? He had a hard time reconciling the image he had carried for years of Heath with the man he had spent the last couple of days with. Court didn't even know if he should broach the topic. For better or worse, Court was blown away.

Another thought creeped in, undermining him. What did Heath expect in exchange? Did he want Court in his debt? He didn't know how to handle this. The doorbell rang, cutting through his spinning thoughts. Court tossed his phone aside. He hoped it wasn't his dad again. Court didn't bother checking his camera. By the time he got it pulled up on his phone, he could have the door open. The immediate rush of joy he felt at the sight of Heath on the other side shocked him speechless.

Heath smiled. He had a cat tucked under one arm and the other hand behind his back. He looked like a butler, presenting him with his daily pet.

Court chuckled. "You know, most men just bring flowers."

A bright smile lit Heath's face. "I believe this is what they call the cat distribution system. He was crying in your yard."

Court plucked Tom from Heath's hold. "Yeah. That's because he's mine. He's just an asshole who likes to escape and try to knock up all the neighborhood cats. Of course, he fails, but that doesn't stop him." He stepped back, letting Heath pass. "I'm surprised he let you pick him up. I wasn't joking. He really is an asshole." He shut the door and set Tom on the floor. When he turned, Heath held a coffee mug with a peace symbol on it and a tiny cactus planted inside.

"This is what I brought. See? It's a peace offering." He pointed at the peace sign. "And it's prickly. Just like me," he said, pointing at the cactus.

Court couldn't stop smiling. His face hurt. "Idiot." He accepted the gift. Court couldn't stop looking at it as he carried it to a nearby shelf. "I'll leave it here where I can be reminded of the day I made amends with a prick."

The sound of Heath's laughter did something to Court's chest. The sensation doubled when he turned and saw the genuine Heath was still with him, smiling and obviously here to stay.

Heath's smile slipped a hair. "Do you mean it?"

"Mean what?"

"Am I forgiven?" He looked like a naughty child, begging for forgiveness. The puppy dog eyes were too much.

"I'm getting there." The sweetest and most heart-stopping smile passed over Heath's lips. Court had to move on. He motioned toward the couch. "You don't have to stand in the middle of the living room. Sit."

Heath moved Court's phone to the coffee table and sat. Court chose the opposite end. For a moment, they sat in uncomfortable silence.

Court couldn't take it. "Why did you do it?"

Heath looked confused as hell. "You'll really have to be more specific. I've done a lot."

An embarrassed chuckle escaped Court. He realized how quick and accusatory his question sounded. He tried to start over with less bursting at the seams. "Why did you pay Dad's debt?"

"Who says I did?"

Court held his stare and chose to wait him out. He didn't want to play games. Unfortunately, the silent staring contest turned hotter than Court expected. Heath's gray eyes were amazing. Everything about him appealed to Court. Always had. It seemed the longing had never stopped.

"I've come to take you away."

Court shook his head. "You're really taking this sixty-day thing seriously."

Heath's expression stayed serious. "No. I paid your dad's debt with Saul, but his credit has been closed across all casinos. When he realizes he's cut off, this'll be the first place he comes, restraining order or not."

"I'm not afraid of my dad. Just tired of him."

"Your dad only owed Saul twenty grand."

Court looked away. "I was afraid of that." Even he heard the dead note in his voice.

"So you know about the drugs?"

Court's arms rose and fell. "It's kind of hard to miss." He stood. "Where are we headed? What do I need to bring?" Court tried to keep his tone light, but he couldn't meet Heath's gaze as he headed for the hall.

Heath stood and intercepted Court before he got away. He stepped into Court's path and hugged him. It seemed it was Heath's go-to move when Court fell apart. God, Court needed it. It was so fucking warm in Heath's arms. Court wanted to rage about losing his parents while they still lived. It didn't matter they breathed, walked, and talked. They were as lost to him as if they had died. They were like dumbass teenagers wanting to fit in with the cool kids. Now he was alone and used up and tired. So fucking tired.

Court didn't know who made the first move. He very much feared it was him. His head turned and their lips bumped. Time froze as they shared each other's air. Old desires raced to the surface. He wanted Heath so fucking badly.

Heath took a step back. "I'm sorry." He looked defeated. "It's like I can't stop proving to you that I'm a terrible person."

Lust made Court's brain slow. "What?"

Heath made a helpless gesture. "You're having a bad time and I'm just—" His hands rose and fell again.

"You're so dumb." Court closed the distance between them and took the kiss he wanted. His soul cried out for all the dreams he had lost. Then Heath hauled him closer, and Court let it go. He wanted this. Heath's kiss scorched him. But the way Heath lovingly held him made Court's eyes burn. He didn't grope Court or try to go further.

"Whoa." Heath's breathless-sounding whisper sounded every bit as blown away as Court felt. "That was... wow."

Court chuckled.

They didn't let go. He couldn't give up the way Heath's arms felt around him.

Heath kissed his cheek. "I fucking hate it, but we still should go. Pack a bag for a few days."

Court didn't know why he didn't argue or even question where they were going. He simply nodded and headed for his bedroom with his brain trapped in a fog of lust. Court had no idea where this thing with Heath was headed. All he knew was he didn't know how to stop.

Heath couldn't stop thinking about that kiss. He wanted to do it again. First, he needed to get Court someplace where he could rest. He wished Court hadn't found his phone, but there wasn't much he could do about that. However, Heath knew exactly where to take Court to forget all his troubles. After calling a friend and snagging a private flight, they were in New Orleans just in time to have gumbo for dinner.

For the hundredth time, Court shook his head at Heath as they sat across from each other at one of Heath's favorite restaurants. "You really just do what you want, don't you?"

The claim made Heath a little uncomfortable. "I thought you'd already concluded I'm spoiled."

Court cocked his head to one side and eyed Heath, as if seeing too much. "I don't know. Obviously, you have access to anything you want, but there's still something about you. Something that keeps you grounded."

Heath stared for half a second before responding. "Not really, no." Court snorted, making Heath smile. Heath chose to be as open with his life as Court had been with his. "There used to be. My grandfather." A smile touched Heath's lips and fell away. "I remember when I was like fourteen, he got a brand-new golf cart. It was his baby. I was messing around and drove that sucker straight into the pond at the golf course."

Court covered his mouth.

Heath couldn't help but chuckle. "Fuck. He was so mad at me. There had honestly been a part of me that thought, meh. He'll just buy a new one. Because like you said, spoiled. He was not amused. When we got home, he stripped my bedroom of everything but my bed. Took away everything. He said I had to earn each and every one of my possessions back one by one with acts of service. One act of service equaled one possession. I whined to my dad about how it would take me forever. I thought he would stick up for me and get my things back. Instead, Dad told me to work smarter and not harder. So, I had a brilliant idea. I would volunteer at a homeless shelter, and I'd have my stuff back by the end of the day." Heath flashed a wry smile. "It was brutal. It was eye opening. But I kept going until I got all my things back and then I kept going because I made friends. So, you know,

I'm still spoiled, but my grandpa tried. Of course, he's dead now, so..."

"Nobody really sees you, do they? Not even you."

Heath didn't know how to respond. He found himself turning subconscious. "Don't worry. I'm still a bad person. You're still allowed to hate me."

Court finished his drink. "Nah. I don't think I will. Are you ready to get out of here? You still have to make it up to me, so I tell everyone you have a little dick and cried afterward."

He was serious. Holy hell. Heath had never wanted anything more. He paid the bill without meeting Court's gaze. Heath knew the neediness was in his eyes. The last couple of days had been killing him. It was stupid how badly he wanted the same man he'd loathed a week ago. He stood and finally met Heath's stare.

"May I walk you back to our room?"

The sweet way Court smiled at his overly gentlemanly tone melted Heath's heart. "I'd like that." Court stood and held Heath's elbow as they headed out and down the street. The air was sticky. Thankfully, the room wasn't far. It was up a set of ridiculously narrow staircases that forced Heath to move behind Court. It was a good view. Once he let Court inside their room, he wasn't sure what to do. Despite Court's words, Heath didn't want to fall on him like a horny bastard. Court deserved better. Heath's body lit like a rocket when Court ended being the one who attacked.

Court's hands were everywhere. He wasn't gentle. Court pushed and tugged at Heath's clothes while their mouths clashed. After a moment of absolute insanity, they were half clothed, and Heath realized he didn't want things to go this way. He didn't want to race to have Court and cheapen the moment. Heath took control, slowing things down. He held Court's face between his hands and savored the way their tongues played as he backed Court toward the bed. When the backs of Court's knees hit the edge of the mattress, he slowly eased Court down before joining him. He worked on divesting them of the remainder of their clothes, but he didn't rush. Heath wanted to have time to memorize every inch of Court. He kissed a path down Court's gorgeous chest and stomach before dragging Court's pants and underwear down his hips. Fuck. Everything about him was perfect for Heath. He fully intended to lick Court's cock. Instead, he found himself on his back, staring at the ceiling, and wondering how he got there. Court had flipped him so fast. Then his clothes were gone, and his dick was in Court's mouth. He wanted to argue, but his throat wouldn't work. Court was fucking masterful. Heath's hips lifted and his muscles clenched. Again, he was ready to blow in Court's mouth so fast, it had to be a world record. Court squeezed Heath's cock at the base, cutting off his orgasm.

A startled cry ripped from Heath.

"Shhh." Court kept Heath's cock squeezed while the building pressure ebbed. Heath wondered if he would go blind. "Trust me," Court whispered as he released him. "I've got you."

Heath couldn't respond. He couldn't fucking breathe. The sensation of nearly blowing like lightning combined with the immediate denial had him spinning. All he could do was pant and stare as he watched Court suit up and lube his cock. Then Court's dick pressed against the tight ring of muscles surrounding his asshole. Heath couldn't even tense. His shock still ran too deep.

"Are you still with me?"

Heath nodded, even though he had no idea.

"Good boy. Open up for me. Don't tense."

Tense? Heath was like a rag doll, waiting to be played with.

Then Court went root deep and Heath lost control. He became the biggest power bottom to ever power. Heath clawed at Court's skin, tugging and pulling. He used Court. Heath fucked himself on Court's body. Court might have pumped inside Heath, but Heath took what he wanted. He likely looked like a madman, tearing at Court to get a single orgasm. Heath already knew he would look back at this night in humiliation because he was a wreck. A needy whore. He whined and whimpered, fighting toward the edge. Court stared down at him, intently watching his every desperate move.

"That's it, beautiful. You're almost there." Court sounded so goddamn calm. Heath was ready to tear off his skin. "Fuck. You look sexy right now. Let me see you blow.

I want it." Goddamn. Heath couldn't disobey. He cried out as cum shot from him. It was the hardest orgasm he had ever experienced. It felt exactly like he had the one Court denied him plus this one together. His body convulsed. Heath babbled words without recollection. Likely, he begged Court to marry him. His soul was rocked. But he still saw Court with a crystal clarity as his face hardened and his teeth bared. He pumped hard inside Heath, riding the same waves as Heath. In the middle of the biggest emotional storm of his life, Heath swore his thoughts were clearer than ever before. He knew exactly why he had hated Court so much. Court belonged to him, and he never wanted to see Court on the arm of another man again, or so help Heath. He would kill him.

There was a reason Court had steered clear of Heath over the past few years, besides the obvious hating him. Court had been so deeply infatuated with Heath at one time, it had definitely turned to love. He was scared shitless of the way Heath made him feel. Court had tried locking down his emotions and simply fucking Heath. But Heath hadn't shut down and Court couldn't unsee every emotion Heath had shown him. Now Heath held Court in a way he had needed for years. Heath had done so through every second of the night and Court had barely slept for fear of losing the arms around him. Why did Heath have to turn out to be so goddamn perfect? Court didn't know if the cracks in his heart were healing or getting wider. Heath threatened every aspect of Court's life, from his job to his sanity.

Soft lips brushed his forehead. "Why are you having such a hard time sleeping? Are you worried about your dad?"

Unexpectedly, Court found himself fighting back tears. There was the perfection again. He didn't know how to shield himself. Court swallowed. "I suppose."

"Hmm." Heath's fingertips trailed up and down Court's spine. "I see. You're drawing a picture in your head of all the ways I'll fuck up your life."

Despite himself, Court smiled. "Maybe."

Heath gently rolled, tucking Court beneath him. He stared down at Court. "You're not wrong."

Court's throat immediately swelled.

Heath didn't stop. "I like you." He chuckled. "Those are words I never thought I'd say, but I do. You're smart, sexy, and amazing. I like you."

"This sounds an awful lot like the 'I like you but' speech."

Heath shook his head. "But yeah, in a way." Court wanted to shove him away and break his nose, but he couldn't move, and Heath didn't stop talking. "I like you, but I can't watch you go out with other guys. Yeah, I know. It's your job and you don't have sex for money, but I want you to be with me." Heath swallowed. He looked truly vulnerable in a way Court had always wanted to see. "I want every-one to know you're mine."

Widening. The cracks in his heart were widening. "That's incredibly sweet and I understand, but—like you said—it's my job. My dad has sucked me dry for years." He desperately wanted Heath to know it wasn't him. Heath wasn't the problem. His fucked-up life was. "I'm barely hang-ing on and I could never afford to simply quit." Defeat washed over him. Until that moment, he hadn't realized exactly how badly he wanted to stop pretending to enjoy being on the arm of old rich men. He wanted to sit home and be in love. Court craved a quiet life.

"Okay. Then let me take care of you."

Court's chest hurt. "I could never ask that of you. You'd always wonder if I only wanted your money."

Heath looked scarily intense. "You're not asking me. I'm asking you. If you need more security than my word, we'll do an indefinite contract. I'm asking you to choose me."

Frustration welled in Court. "It's been one night."

"It's more than that and you know it."

The conviction in Heath's eyes couldn't be missed. He honestly wanted this. "A trial period."

A smile exploded across Heath's face and Court already knew he had lost. "You won't regret me."

"That's not what I'm worried about." Court really needed Heath to understand. "It's one thing for people to see me on your arm at the golf course. It's a whole other for people to see us as a real couple. People won't envy you. I'm still the whore you painted me to be in school in the eyes of everyone in the community. I'm not one of you. Not really. I'm just a high-priced toy. How long until you're embarrassed by that?"

Heath kissed him. It was sweet. "Have some faith in me." Their kiss deepened and Court's walls fell. God help him. He believed, and he had never been more terrified in his life.

CHAPTER SEVEN

LIFE TURNED QUIETER THAN Court expected. His parents were strangely silent. Court had no clue why Heath bothered paying Court's house payment. He hadn't been back in the five months since they returned from New Orleans, except to grab clothes and Tom. Tom prowled Heath's huge house like he owned the place now. He definitely treated Heath like he owned him. If Heath was bothered by his furry houseguest, he never showed it. There were simply days of peace and nights of fire with the occasional obligatory social outing. And sports. Jesus. So many fucking sports. Heath played everything. He was the most athletic person Court had ever met. Of course, that was how he had caught Court's eye in school. Honestly, it wasn't hard to watch Heath's sexy body flex and move with every play he made.

Court chewed the side of his nail and watched Heath run, dribble, and elbow his way from one end of the basketball court to the other. He jumped to make a shot. Court stood. Someone checked Heath, knocking him to the floor. Court winced as Heath's body hit the unforgiving wooden floor. A whistle blew.

"That's two."

Heath popped to his feet. His gaze shot Court's way. He was all smiles. When he winked, Court's heart sighed. Heath held up one finger, asking for a moment from the ref. Since it was purely locals being overly competitive, they allowed Heath to jog his way. Sweat ran down Heath's face.

"I need a kiss for good luck."

Court curled his nose, but he couldn't stop smiling.

Heath didn't give him a chance to say no. He snagged Court's face and placed loud, wet kisses all over Court's face, dripping sweat all over him in the process. He didn't stop until Court laughed and begged for mercy.

"There. Now I can't miss." He jogged away just as quickly as he had attacked.

Court smiled like an idiot, and he couldn't stop. Sure enough, Heath made both shots. Court watched with pride and so many other emotions, he forgot where he was. All he saw was Heath. Heath was proud to be with him. He never missed an opportunity to make him feel special while also letting everyone see they were together. For real. A real couple. Court was a little ashamed to admit he hadn't actually signed anything after the sixty-day contract ended. Heath's lawyer and accountant had gotten with Court's lawyer and accountant. Court's bills were paid. Money went into his account. Heath always took care of everything to the point that Court never even thought about it. He didn't need a contract. Court didn't want one. In fact, since he hadn't bailed out his dad this last time, for once, he had a truly hefty savings account. If he didn't get another dime from Heath, he could afford to find another job. One that wouldn't ruin them. There was such a weight gone from his chest. No one could possibly understand. He needed this normalcy.

"It's been a while."

Court startled at the unexpected words against his ear. He turned. Portland stood behind him. Court patted his chest. "Hey. You startled me. What are you doing here?"

Portland shrugged. "There're a lot of bets on this game. You know I can't miss an opportunity to win."

That was weird, but the elite were a strange bunch. "Are you betting for or against Heath?"

Portland's light blue gaze moved over Court's face. "You've changed since the last time we spoke. I thought you were dead set against being trapped in a contract with Heath."

Court shrugged. "I'm not in a contract."

A smile stretched Portland's lips. It wasn't exactly comfortable. "Good. That means you're free to attend the charity cruise with me later this year."

"Actually, no." Court winced. He didn't want to sound harsh. "I'm not free. Not anymore." He cleared his throat. "Not ever. I'm out."

Portland had a closed expression Court always found a bit disturbing. He liked Portland, but the guy was still waters. Court had never been exactly sure what lay beneath. "So, you're in an actual rela-tionship with Heath."

It wasn't a question, but Court chose to treat it as one. "Yes."

"How are you supporting yourself?"

Court found the question a little rude, but he let it go. "I get by."

"I see."

Fuck. Things were getting more than slightly uncomfortable. There was some-thing in Portland's tone. Court didn't understand. A loud buzzer nearly made Court jump out of his skin. He turned. The game was over. Heath was headed his way, wearing his biggest smile. He had won. Of course he had. Court glanced over to commiserate with Portland. He was gone. Court let it go and focused on

Heath. The entire encounter with Portland had been odd as hell. Court didn't know why, but it dropped a seed of worry in the back of Court's brain. It didn't take long for Heath to make him forget.

Heath felt so light—like he breathed freer than ever before. He had always filled his life with nonstop activities so he wouldn't go insane. Now he had someone to share his life with and he still went nonstop, but now he smiled everywhere he went.

"What do you want to do now?"

Court looked exasperated. "Aren't you tired?"

Heath twirled Court on the way to the car like they were dancing. "Nope." He wrapped his arms around Court and dipped before stealing a bunch of quick kisses. "I've got you. I'm on top of the world. Do you want to get something to eat?" He walked, still holding Court against his chest, so he was basically dragging him. Court was smiling. That was all that mattered to Heath.

"You probably are starving after that workout. What are you in the mood for?"

Heath waggled his eyebrows at Court.

Court punched him in the arm. "Idiot."

His phone buzzed. He blew out a raspberry. "Hold that thought." Heath freed one arm only long enough to check his phone. He barely skimmed the text before shoving the device back in his coat pocket and returning to annoying Court. "Oh no. Change of plans. We've been summoned to dinner with my parents."

Court looked horrified. "We?"

"Yes, we." He kissed the corner of Court's mouth, being as lovingly gross and obnoxious as possible. "I don't keep you a secret. Nom. Nom." He chewed Court's bottom lip. Then he set him aside as if he hadn't been driving the guy crazy. He unlocked the car and opened the passenger side door, motioning Court inside. "Would you like a ride, little boy? I have candy."

"Oh no. I'm not supposed to talk to strangers." Court jumped in. "But candy? Yum."

With a laugh, Heath closed the door and circled the car. He had been ridiculously happy since New Orleans and it never got old.

Court turned serious when Heath climbed behind the wheel. "Am I dressed okay? Should we go home and change first?"

Heath shook his head. "You're adorable." He stole a kiss. It turned heated without a plan. Heath simply felt too much. He forced himself to pull away. "You're perfect. We're just going to their house. Nothing formal." Heath knew Court was comfortable in almost all situations, except where he expected to be judged harshly. In this case, Heath didn't care what his parents thought, and it was time for them to recognize Court as a part of his life. Heath had been slowly moving him in. It was almost funny the way even Court didn't notice. Heath wanted to laugh. Court had walked past the bookshelf from his living room for three weeks without realizing it.

"Come on." He kissed the tip of Court's nose. "You've got this."

"If you say so." Court already sounded defeated, and they hadn't gotten there yet.

Heath shook his head and backed from his parking spot. Truthfully, he didn't know what to expect. They had avoided the major holidays with his family, since his parents had decided to do a European tour as a gift to each other, so Court had been spared this until now. Unfortunately, his parents were either extremely pretentious or totally oblivious to other people, or both. He wasn't sure what he hoped would happen, but it was best to get it out of the way. Court would have to meet them, eventually.

It bothered him how tightly Court held his hand. Heath was determined this would go well for his sake. Court already had his own parents seemingly set against him. This likely looked daunting as hell. Thankfully, his mom was all smiles as they came through the door. She greeted Court warmly. Heath breathed a sigh of relief.

"You have a lovely home."

Sharon smiled. "Thank you. I believe your mother used the same decorator." His mom took Court's arm and led him to the table. "You got here just in time. Dinner has just been served."

Court wore his most charming smile. The one he used professionally. Heath hated it. That smile gnawed at his gut. As he sat, he glanced around the table and a sadness washed over him. He had added a new player to their absolutely fake family. Court squeezed his hand beneath the table. Heath's shoulders eased. Court was still real. They were in this together. He ate and made conversation. It was the usual bland stuff about the weather, golf, and their friends. Court's hand on his knee saved him. That and the wine. His parents drank with obvious purpose, loosening their usual stiff personalities.

By the time dessert rolled around, they had consumed way more alcohol than usual, and his mother had already excused herself to rest. His dad polished off the last of their fourth bottle.

"We still have dessert to finish. Why don't you grab us another bottle, son? A red this time."

Court flashed him a sweet smile.

Heath grabbed the empty bottle so he could trash it on the way to the wine cellar. As he passed his dad, he noticed he looked a little too friendly. Something about his expression gave Heath pause. The moment he was out of sight, Heath hesitated before choosing to stick close and listen.

"Okay. Now that we're alone. How much to make you go away?"

Court's nervous laughter filled the air. "I'm sorry, what?"

"You are embarrassing our family. I don't care what you do to support yourself, but do it elsewhere. So, give me a number. What'll it take to break your contract?"

Heath couldn't move. His chest hurt.

"We don't have a contract. I'm with Heath because I want to be."

His dad scoffed. "We don't have time for you to lie to me to negotiate a higher price. Just throw out a number so I can write you a check and you can be gone by the end of the night."

Court's voice hardened. "I can't be bought. If you have a problem with our relationship, you need to address it with your son."

"If you truly care about him, you won't make me go that far. You either accept a check now or get nothing because I will disown him before I allow him to blow this family's fortune on a gold-digging whore."

Something inside Heath snapped. His feet carried him back into the room. He slammed the empty bottle back on the table with enough force, he was surprised it didn't crack. "I know I didn't hear what I think I just heard." Heath stared at his dad with murder in his eyes and heart.

"I'm sorry, Heath, but this is too much. Your grandfather would—"

Heath sliced his hand through the air, cutting him off. "There's absolutely nothing you can say to me right now. For the first time in my life, I'm genuinely happy. You trying to ruin that tells me everything I need to know. We are done."

Heath grabbed Court's hand and headed for the door.

His dad was hot on his heels. "Don't do anything stupid. I was only looking out for my father's legacy."

Heath didn't slow.

Court didn't make a sound until they were in the car. "I don't want this."

Heath's head snapped around. He would not let Court blow up what they had built over his shitty family. "Don't you start. I would rather have you than all the fake-ass family in the world. You are the best thing that's ever happened to me. I have never been this happy. You can't take that from me because of them." Heath took a breath. He realized shouting made him sound like a controlling asshole. Truthfully, he was terrified. He tried again. Calmer this time. "Seriously. Please don't do this."

Court looked on the verge of tears. "How long will it take before you resent me after your parents cut you off? When you're out here working a job because of me, you'll hate me."

Despite everything, a smile exploded across Heath's face. "Baby, everything you witnessed tonight is theater. My parents never wanted kids. They only had me to please my grandfather. Thankfully, I was a boy to carry on the family name so they could stop with me. But if it was up to them, they would've walked away from me the day I turned eighteen with their obligation complete." Heath kissed Court's nose before he continued. He couldn't stop himself. His heart needed comforting. "There's a reason we lived in this house with my grandfather until he died. My grandfather's house. My dad is a black hole when it comes to money and my grandfather couldn't trust him. He refused to support him unless we stayed under his roof where he could keep an eye on every cent. Everything is mine. My grandfather left it all to me. Without me, they'll be in the streets. I control every dime. My grandfather trusted me to keep my dad from running everything into the ground. My dad can't do shit to me."

Court looked stunned.

Heath kept his finances private because that was what old money did. But no one would be cutting him off and Court didn't have a damn thing to worry about.

"Are we good? Because really. You're the only real thing in my life. I'm so fucking in love with you that I'm pretty sure I'll just wither away and die if you walk away."

Court's features softened. "You love me?"

Heath shrugged. "I thought it was obvious, but maybe not since you just planned to dump me."

Court leaned across the console and brushed a light kiss across Heath's lips. "I love you too. If you honestly think you won't regret me over tonight, then I'm not going anywhere."

A smile had stretched Heath's lips at Court saying he loved him and only got bigger by the second. "I swear. You mean everything to me."

Court buckled his seatbelt. "Then we might want to go home. Your mom is headed this way."

Heath threw the car in reverse without another thought. He hadn't been joking. Heath was done with his parents. He would keep up their household, because that was what his grandfather would have wanted. Otherwise, they had burned this bridge. Heath chose love.

CHAPTER EIGHT

COURT'S STOMACH WAS IN knots. The attack from Heath's father had come so swiftly, catching him completely off guard. The night had taken so many twists and turns. Court might have felt totally off balance if it wasn't for that goddamn I love you. The intensity that bled from Heath as he had made that confession still warmed Court's skin. Until he heard the words and said them back, Court hadn't realized how true they were. The peace and happiness Heath had brought into his life had a name. They would be okay.

As Heath's gorgeous house came into view, Court immediately felt like coming home. He was deep. This was real. He had never stood a chance of things being any other way. Heath did something he never did as he turned into the driveway. He hit the button to close the metal gate at the end of the driveway. It was obvious he expected his parents would follow.

He flashed Court an apologetic smile. "I'll need to find the other remote so you can freely come and go, but for tonight..."

Court brought Heath's hand to his mouth and kissed it. "I know. It's fine."

After pulling into the garage, Heath dug out his phone and started blocking numbers. He didn't even wait until they were inside. Court hated that things had come to this. It was one hundred percent his fault. Heath's parents weren't wrong. Court was an embarrassment. He had tried warning Heath he would be. It didn't matter Court had never had sex for money. His business was perceived that way. He honestly didn't want this for Heath, but he wouldn't be the one who ended things. Court was selfish. He wanted Heath too badly and he would never hurt him like that.

With his blocking spree out of the way, they headed inside, hand in hand. They had left the kitchen light on. The place smelled like apple pie. He didn't know why. Court assumed it was something the cleaning crew did, but it smelled like home. He didn't know what was going on with him, but he felt too much tonight. Something about them felt unsettled. He kept waiting for the other shoe to drop. Apparently, being overly sentimental was how he coped. He couldn't stop staring at Heath with all the love in his heart.

Heath dug through a drawer in the kitchen.

Court watched, hating the silence. Everything inside the kitchen was blue. A gorgeous, perfect for him blue. This was his home. His chest hurt. That other place with his name on the deed was like a distant memory. Tom weaved through his legs before moving to scratch at Heath's jeans. Absently, Heath picked him up, kissed his head, and then set him on the counter.

Court smiled. This was a family. The first real one he'd had in a long time. "Cats shouldn't be on the counter."

Tom flicked his tail at him.

Heath set him back on the floor. "Daddy said no counter time. He doesn't want your fur all over his kitchen. He's right. That's why you can't eat at everybody's house."

Court's throat swelled. Heath called it his kitchen. Court was all the way in his feelings, and it wasn't necessarily a good thing. He desperately wanted the home Heath offered. Court wanted the family. He fucking hated feeling alone in the world. Something felt unsettled.

Heath turned with his head down, eyeing the items in his hand. "You already have a key to this door, but you need one for the front, just in case. So, here's that one. You already have the garage remote, but here's the one for the gate. We should probably start using it. Between your parents and mine, we'll be lucky if they don't rob our house every day." He lifted his chin and met Court's stare when Court didn't immediately take the items. A line appeared between his eyebrows. "Are you okay?"

Court swallowed. "You called it our house."

Heath's expression cleared. "Oh. Is it not?"

He could barely breathe. "I'd like it to be." The pride he swallowed to utter that sentence nearly choked him.

Heath set the key and remote on the counter and pulled Court into his arms.

"I know, baby. It's been a hell of a night." He kissed Court's temple. "This is your home. Come here." He turned Court in his arms, facing him toward the wall. "Does anything look familiar?"

Court started to scoff at the asinine question until he realized he stared at a wooden sideboard that had been his kitchen. "What the hell?"

Heath laughed against his ear. "More than half your furniture is here and you haven't even noticed." He gently turned Court to face him again. His eyes looked soft but worried. "I haven't wanted to pressure you, but this is your home. Not only do you belong here, but I'd feel safer if you stayed here. Your dad is unpredictable. Plus, I love you and I just want you here."

"I love you." Court honestly thought he might cry.

A smile snapped to Heath's lips. "Was that an agreement?"

Court nodded.

Heath drew him closer. "Then you should definitely kiss me to seal the deal. Don't you think?"

Court touched his lips to Heath's. That was all it took for his love to turn them into an inferno. Their tongues played while they fought to get closer. Heath stole his shirt before lifting him onto the counter. He kissed a path down Court's body as he tore open Court's jeans, setting his cock free. Court fought for air as Heath swallowed his erection. While leaned back on his hands, he stared down at Heath, watching every second. Heath looked like he was in heaven and that fucked hard with Court's head. He had felt desired many times in his life, but never to the extent Heath showed.

Heath sucked and used his hands to pleasure Court. Court moaned as he fought to reach the explosion Heath's mouth promised. Before he got there, he found himself on his feet, face pressed to the counter with nothing but coconut oil for lube. A loud moan burst from Court as Heath impaled him. He clung to the counter for dear life.

"That's it. Oh, my god. Fuck me." They were both vers and Heath was unpredictable. It was sexy as hell, never knowing if he would beg for Court's cock or take him hard. They were perfect.

"Paint this kitchen floor with your cum." Heath bit his shoulder. "It's yours. You can treat it however you want."

Fuck. Every word he said added to Court's insanity. He wanted to jack off and take his pleasure, but he wanted Heath to make him come even more. Court focused on Heath's perfect angle and the pressure climbing his shaft. When he blew, cries tore from him like stuck on repeat. There wasn't a single thought left in his head. He was all love and nothing more. Then flashes of them flowed through his mind like watching their life together on film. Heath cried out his name against Court's shoulder. All Court could do was cling to the counter and try not to bawl like a baby. He had known this man almost his entire life. Court felt closer to him than anyone in the world. For the first time in years, Court believed he could have a beautiful life. He had never felt more humbled by fate.

Heath couldn't stop touching Court. He didn't think he could be blamed. The night had been a huge emotional roller-coaster. But in their bed with Court in his arms, everything felt perfect. He wasn't upset about his parents. All he felt was relief, honestly. He didn't have to fake it anymore. A small part of him wanted to scream and rage each time he thought about the things his dad had said, but Court had turned him down. Not only that, he had been outraged at the idea of being paid to dump Heath. Not once had he doubted Court's reasons to be with him, but it still felt good. Then Court had finally recognized he lived here. Heath genuinely felt over the moon. He couldn't sleep. Heath wanted to feel every inch of Court and memorize every detail. He felt half insane with obsession. No one could truly understand, though. His life had been totally empty before Court filled him with happiness and love. Heath was addicted.

"I'm a little worried about what my dad will do when my house goes on the market. No doubt he'll see dollar signs and lose his mind."

Heath kissed his forehead, trying to reassure him. "I'll contact a real estate friend of mine. He can do a private sale. Hell, he might be interested in buying it. He's been buying up a lot of property around here lately."

"Sounds good." Court kissed his chest. He sounded completely at peace with no longer having his old house. "When I have all that extra money, I can take you on a special trip. The way you did for me when my parents were the problem."

Heath knew Court was trying to be sweet, but his claim bugged Heath. "I'm sorry. We've been so whirlwind, I haven't thought to make sure your bank account is good."

Court went up onto one elbow. He looked aggravated. "I wasn't trying to get money out of you. In fact, I was trying to do something for you. You take care of me just fine."

Heath used his thumb to soothe away the line between Court's eyebrows. "Stop. I know you. You don't have a greedy bone in your body."

Court snorted. "Well, I might have one."

Heath accepted Court's joke for the olive branch it was. "It's okay. I like that one, but don't try to change the subject. You'll have a long, frustrating life if you worry over every dollar I spend on you. I want to spend the rest of my life with you. Do you want one of those ridiculous marriages where we keep our finances separate and bicker over how we split each bill? That's crazy."

He felt Court relax. "Honestly? As long as I get to have you, I don't care. If I have to go flip burgers so I can split the electric bill, that's what I'll do."

Heath rolled, pinning Court beneath him. "No." Even he felt how intense he became. He tried toning it down. "No flipping burgers. No dragging yourself to work. Your job is to be mine. I didn't mean to sound like I think of you as an object. You know what I mean." He hoped Court understood, anyhow.

"I get it." Court tucked a hair behind Heath's ear. The love in his expression was nearly Heath's undoing. "You're mine. I'm not all athletic like you, but I'll still bite a bitch if they try to take you."

A bark of laughter burst from Heath. "That's a real threat. Your dad is a dentist. You've got good teeth."

The way Court shook with laughter had Heath smiling so hard, his face hurt.

"That was hard work for him too. I have fat kid tendencies and love candy."

Heath shrugged. He kissed Court's neck, nibbling his skin. "I don't care if you get fat. There'll just be more of you to love."

Court chuckled. "You go too much. I could never get fat just trying to keep up with you. Oh, god. Don't stop that."

Heath sucked Court's neck, doing exactly as told. He never got enough. As long as Court would let him enjoy his body, Heath was there.

Court's cellphone rang.

Heath groaned. "Dad probably called around and got your number. Fuck. I didn't think about that." He grabbed Court's phone, determined to block his parents there too. He didn't recognize the number. "Yeah. I don't know who this is." He passed the phone to Court.

Court looked confused. He answered and immediately switched the call to speakerphone. "Hello?"

"It's Mom. I'm at the hospital with your dad." Court sat straight up, nearly head-butting Heath in the process. "What? What happened?"

She sniffed. It was obvious she was crying. "It's really bad. Can you please come? He's in room four in the trauma center."

Court scrambled from the bed. "Yeah. Give me a minute. I'm on my way." He didn't even say goodbye.

Heath was right behind him. They dressed side by side. Court looked pale. Heath had a bad feeling in his gut. No matter how terrible Court's parents were, he loved them and he couldn't save them from themselves. Heath prayed they hadn't found a new way to wreck Court. Heath had just put him back together.

CHAPTER NINE

EVEN THOUGH HE WAS headed for the hospital, there was still a part of Court that wondered if this was a game. He honestly didn't put anything past his dad. On the flip side of things, there were so many ways his dad could turn up dead. Overdose. Car crash while high. Finally getting his comeuppance with the wrong person he had crossed. He didn't know what to expect. Court didn't know why he cared. The closer he got to the room, the less he wanted to go. Maybe he was coldhearted. Possibly, he had finally been completely used up. No matter the reason, his initial worry and terror were gone, leaving behind an odd ambivalence. He was here, though. Court might as well find out why.

The last thing he expected, even though he didn't know why, was to find his father sitting up in bed, looking relatively fine. His gray-tinged blond hair stood in every direction and his eye was black. Otherwise, his mom looked worse than him from all the crying.

"This is bad?" Even Court heard the incredulous note in his voice.

His mother wailed. "Look at his legs," she demanded between obnoxious cries.

"Look what they did to him. How is he supposed to work like that?"

His dad's legs were both tightly wrapped, as if possibly broken. He looked guilty, which only furthered Court's annoyance. They hadn't let Heath come back with him to the room since he wasn't family. Court wished like hell he was there. He had a bad feeling he would need Heath to stop him from pouncing. His eye twitched. Then a cold calm settled over him.

"Well, I imagine he was too high at the time to have felt any of this." He held his dad's stare. "So, which debt got you into this?"

His dad looked away.

Court realized he felt nothing except tired. "It seems it's time for you to sell the house. You've got nothing else, and I'm done. Honestly, I'm surprised you lasted this long." He heard how cold he sounded. There was no regret or sadness in him. These weren't the same people who raised him. They had let money change them into strangers.

"You can't leave us without a house. Call Portland. He'll do anything for a night with you. He's always taken care of you in the past."

Court felt sick. Of all the insults and insinuations that had been flung his way over the past few years, he honestly had never felt like a whore. He knew his boundaries, even if no one else saw them. But in that moment, Court realized something so monumental, it broke him. His parents thought he whored for them, and they were fine as long as they got everything they wanted. Court didn't speak. He simply walked away. His mom's high-pitched wails followed him, but he didn't truly hear a thing. All he wanted was to get back to where love lived. His heart shattered and then hardened with every step. For the first time, he fully realized his parents were gone. All he had in this world was Heath. The man who Court had spent his life stuck between loving and hating was the only person who gave a single fuck about him. Court would pour everything into him.

Heath looked worried when he spotted Court. He stood. "Is everything okay?"

"I'm done." He took Heath's hand and headed for the door. Thankfully, Heath didn't ask questions. He simply followed Court's lead.

Inside the car, Heath didn't start it right away. He stared at nothing for a minute before finally meeting Court's stare. "I'm sorry."

A sad smile tugged at Court's lips. "Me too, but I'll be okay."

Heath kissed his hand. "Damn right."

For a moment, they simply stared at each other. Court didn't know what to do or say. It was just them now. All it had taken was one night to show them they were all they needed, but Court didn't know how to put into words the way Heath had saved him. He didn't know how to express the way he felt—deep in his soul—that he had always wanted Heath, because they were meant for each other.

But once again, Heath ended up being the one with the words. "Do you remember the night we played spin the bottle?"

A loud snort burst from Court. "Vividly."

"Good." Heath bit his bottom lip, looking slightly guilty. "I called you over to play with us."

Court smiled. "I recall."

"I stopped that bottle on you on the sly."

Court couldn't help but laugh. "You did not."

"I did."

For a second, Court floundered. He wanted to call bullshit again, but he hadn't been joking. Court recalled every second of that night with crystal clarity. His brain locked on the moment that bottle landed on him. Court had watched that bottle spin with a desperation of his entire life riding on the outcome. Damn. Heath had stopped it. It had been sly. If Court hadn't been watching so intently, he would have missed it. At the time, he had merely thought Heath had dropped the cigarette he had been handing to his friend, but the drop had been exact, stopping the bottle on Court.

His gaze snapped to Heath.

A wry smile touched Heath's lips. "I wasn't oblivious. Like I said, you went by a different name back then, and obviously, you looked completely different, but I saw you. No one else stared at me the way you did. You always had so much heat in your eyes. It was a horny teen's dream. Why do you think I blew so fast the moment you touched me? I knew you'd burn me to the ground, but I was a shithead, and you were nobody. I didn't know how to get you alone without..."

"Humiliating yourself," Court finished for him.

Heath winced. "Like I said, I was a shit-head."

"You actually weren't."

Heath looked confused as fuck.

Court didn't make him ask. "It was never your athleticism or popularity that caught my eye. You were nice. I know you don't remember, but I recall every tiny detail. You used to position your body in the locker room so the other guys didn't look my way and make fun of my weight while changing for gym. You always in-cluded people who never got included in anything. I noticed all those things. In fact, I suppose that was one of the biggest reasons I was crushed by the cruelty. In my head, I'd built you up to be this amazing guy. It was a hard drop from the pedestal I had built for you. Funnily enough, it turns out you really are amazing. Life is funny." It was absolutely crazy to him that Heath had wanted him before Court changed himself to unrecognizable from his fat days.

"We were one hundred percent meant to be. All this other shit is terrible, but we've always had each other, even when we didn't realize it. Just because we went our separate ways for a while and I forgot about those days, everything looks so clear now. It was always us."

"Thank god." Court had never meant anything more. Without Heath, he had no idea where he would be right then, but he knew it would be terrible.

Heath leaned across the car and stole a kiss. "I love you. Do you trust me to make everything better?"

Court couldn't help but smile. "Always."

"Good." Heath settled back and started the car. "Close your eyes. Get some rest. I've got you."

Court did as told. He knew Heath had him. They always had each other.

They had to move on with their lives. There was too much drama. It felt like they couldn't simply be a happy couple without some over-the-top bullshit. Heath needed to put his foot down. It seemed as if he had been calling in every favor he had since they started dating. Court was worth it. Heath grabbed his phone and texted Noir before pulling from the parking lot. Since the hospital hadn't let him go back with Court, Heath had reached out to Noir. He knew if anyone had heard the gossip, it was him. Heath hadn't been wrong. Drue's debts had come calling. Apparently, that was exactly what Court needed to finally fully walk away. Unfortunately, he didn't think walking away guaranteed Court would be safely left out of the equation if Drue didn't find a way to pay. That meant Heath had to once and for all solidify Court's position in the community. He would no longer be Drue Langley's son.

Court would be Heath Overton's husband. That mattered more than because of money and stature. Heath was best friends with Prince Noir. There were some people no one dared fuck with. Noir was at the absolute top of that list.

Heath drove on autopilot while plotting the best he could with very little time. Tonight, they needed sleep. Court had left his phone with Heath while he visited his father. Heath had used the opportunity to block all Court's family contacts. So at least they should have a phone call-free night. They needed more than that. Court looked mentally and physically exhausted. Heath wasn't far behind him.

He pulled into a circular drive and put the car in park.

Court's eyes shot open. He blinked at their surroundings as a royal guard opened his door. "Where are we?"

"Prince Noir's," Heath answered as he climbed from the car and passed his keys to a different guard. They would know better than him how to keep his vehicle protected overnight. He took Court's hand and headed for the door. Noir waited for them. Court looked half dead but still awed. Even though they ran in the same circles, Heath doubted Noir had ever spoken to Court. One of them or not, Court would be beneath him.

Thankfully, Noir didn't look as cold as he could be tonight. He focused on Heath. "You made it faster than I expected."

Heath chuckled. "I'm fucking exhausted."

Noir's light green gaze shifted Court's way. "You look tired too. I've had a room opened for you. You have nothing to worry about here."

Even though Court was visibly confused, he still managed a sweet smile. "Thank you."

Noir nodded. "I'll leave you to it. Ajax will show you the way."

"Thank you."

Noir gave him a quick hug. "Of course. You'd do the same for me."

Noir's huge, long-time guard led the way through Noir's enormous estate. Only because Heath had been there countless times did he know his way around.

Court didn't speak until they were alone in a guest room. "I take it we're staying the night."

Heath flashed Court a smile before turning back the covers on the cozy-looking bed. He patted the mattress. "Not only will no one bother us for the rest of the night, Noir's guards are some of the best in the world. You're completely safe here."

Court didn't move. "You think I'm not safe?"

Heath didn't respond.

Court's shoulders fell. He took off his shoes and walked to the bed, looking defeated.

Heath stopped him before he could climb beneath the covers and helped him strip. "This is just for a couple of days, at most. Honestly, I'm hoping it's just for tonight. It depends on you." He paused in stealing Court's clothes to hold his stare. "It depends on how quickly you're willing to marry me."

For a moment, Court merely looked stunned before his expression turned sad. "I never wanted you to be forced to marry me. You don't deserve this."

Irritation flared inside him. "Are you being serious right now?" He angrily divested Court of the remainder of his clothes. "After everything we've talked about. Every confession. You still think I don't want to marry you?" His gaze snapped to Court's with every bit of rage he felt. "You're a fucking idiot."

To his surprise, Court smiled. He cupped Heath's face. "But I'm your idiot." Court kissed his nose. "I'm ready to get married whenever you are. Nothing would make me happier."

Heath's shoulders relaxed. He realized his exhaustion made him a bit touchy. "Sorry." He turned sheepish. "I love you. Can we please get some sleep?"

Court kissed him and dutifully climbed into bed. Heath stripped before turning off the lights and joining him. As Court molded against him, finding his usual sleeping position, Heath realized he was smiling. Somehow, it had been the best and worst night of his life. He had lost a lot and gained even more. A win was a win. He would take it.

CHAPTER TEN

TRUTH BE TOLD, PORTLAND found black-jack tedious as hell. Unfortunately, casinos were the perfect place to conduct business. No one batted an eye over large sums of money changing hands and law enforcement didn't dare interfere with casino business. No one saw anything on the gambling floor.

Lucas slid into the chair to Portland's right. The lanky redhead dropped a black bag at Portland's feet.

Portland didn't bother looking inside. "I take it things went well."

Lucas motioned to the dealer for cards. "After some convincing, it seems Langley had equity in his home."

Portland grunted. He honestly didn't care if Drue ended up dead or homeless. Money was owed. Someone would find it.

Lucas played his hand before speaking again. "What finally convinced you to collect? He's been deeper."

Cold jealousy poured through Portland's veins. "He's gotten a little too comfortable taking advantage. I doubt he has anything left after the house. My good graces are gone."

Lucas nodded. "Especially since his son is off limits."

Portland ground his back teeth for a moment. The way Court had watched Heath during that game still made his eye twitch. He needed to ramp up the pressure. Court had to come crawling back. "Maybe not any longer. The moment Drue's back in my debt, we'll see what Court will be wiling to do."

Lucas looked his way. He stayed silent until Portland met his stare. Lucas looked perplexed. "What do you mean? Court married Heath. Noir will never let you touch him and I'm sure as fuck not ending up like Rico. You've never seen Noir in a frenzy. I might be crazy, but I'm not stupid."

Portland stopped listening after hearing Court married Heath. His pulse pounded in his ears. "He married Heath?" Even Portland heard the dead note in his voice.

"Yeah." Lucas looked worried—like he thought Portland might strike him. "Yesterday at Noir's estate. It was a small ceremony, but I thought you would've heard by now."

The urge to tear the entire building down was nearly blinding. Portland had never felt so much helpless rage in his life. He needed to make someone pay, but Court was forever out of his reach.

A delicious scent wafted over him. "Excuse me." The soft voice had Portland's head whipping around.

A man leaned past him, wearing a dealer's uniform. His focus was locked on the table's dealer. "Sorry. I left my bag."

The dealer glanced below the table and found a small, clear plastic tote bag. He passed it the interloper's way.

Brown eyes swung his way. A sassy smile appeared. His gaze dropped to Portland's mouth and returned to hold his stare. "Excuse me. I didn't mean to invade your space."

He looked too much like Court at the wrong time. Except he didn't look a damn thing like Court, but Portland's brain still locked on him in the same toxic way. He was the same build and close to Court's age. That was enough. The guy turned away as quickly as he appeared. Portland snatched up the bag at his feet and stood. Someone had to feel his wrath. With Court out of his reach, anyone would do. A slight brunette who smelled too good for his own good would do as much as the next person. Portland would get his pound of flesh. It didn't matter to him who paid.

Heath didn't want to change Court. He enjoyed having Court on the sidelines of every little ridiculous sport he played. Heath liked knowing he had the hottest spouse cheering him on. This was fun too.

Heath leaped out of the way as Court lobbed another tennis ball his way, hitting it as hard as possible. Court laughed, enjoying the torment.

"You're supposed to be practicing your swing. Why are you running from the ball?"

Heath ran in a circle, acting completely ridiculous just so he could listen to

Court's laughter some more. "I don't want to practice today. I want to have fun."

Court threw a ball and hit him with it. "Then why are we here? I thought you wanted to win this weekend's tournament."

"I just want to play all day."

Court snorted. "You're ridiculous."

Heath stopped running and locked eyes with Court. "Am I?"

"Oh, no." Court looked every bit as worried as he should.

Heath was in the mood to be dumb. "Oh, yes." He prowled toward Court.

"Shit." Court wasn't quick enough.

Heath jumped the net and tackled him. Peals of laughter tore through the air as Heath headed for the building, carrying Court. Heads turned their way. Some people smiled while others just shook their heads. Heath didn't care. He paid his country club dues just like the next guy. While he had stopped paying his parents' membership so they wouldn't run into one another, he knew his constant antics always got back to them. Heath was no longer worried about old money's reputation. Happiness ruled everything he did now. Nothing mattered as much as his husband's happiness.

Someone held the door open for Heath. He didn't look their way. "Thank you." Heath scanned the hallway. Locker rooms were on the right. Racquetball courts were on the left. Heath veered into the locker room. A guy mopping the floor eyed Heath, mouth agape, as he carried a laughing Court inside. Heath nodded at him like he didn't have his husband tucked under his arm. He paused and eyed the room. A door stood open with cleaning supplies filling the shelf.

Heath turned the worker's way and handed him a folded bill from his pocket. "You saw nothing." He carried Court into the broom closet and closed the door.

Darkness engulfed them. He set Court on his feet. "Here we go. Five minutes in the closet. What should we do?"

Court crowded his space. "I don't know. If memory serves, you should press your erection against me, so I know you're willing."

Heath leaned against the wall and snagged Court's hips. He hauled him forward, so Court felt how hard Heath was for him. "I stay this way with you around. You should know that by now."

With an evil chuckle, Court shaped Heath's erection through his shorts. "Yum. Is that for me?"

There was so much love swelling Heath's chest, he thought he might burst. He never knew where to go with the over-abundance of pure joy. All he knew was he couldn't keep his hands to himself. "Everything is always for you." Even to his ears, Heath sounded aroused. He leaned in to take the kiss he wanted.

Instead, Court dropped to his knees. Heath remembered this part too well. With the slightest tug of clothing, Heath's dick was in Court's mouth. In some circles, five minutes in the closet was known as five minutes in heaven. That was how it felt, except there was no way he would last that long. There was talent and then there was raw hunger. Court wanted Heath's cock exactly where it was. That was such a mind fuck. Heath bit his bottom lip to keep from moaning as he rode Court's tongue. Court kept the perfect pace, humming around Heath's erection like he tasted the most delicious food. Heath never stood a chance. In no time, he gasped as his soul flew. He saw stars as pulse after pulse of ecstasy shook him. The wall kept him upright while he soared through the bliss.

Court kissed his way up Heath's body, fixing his clothes as he went. When he reached Heath's lips, he spent a moment exploring Heath's mouth while waiting for Heath to catch his breath.

Court's mouth moved to Heath's ear. "No more practice today. It's time to go home where I can fuck you as roughly as I want while you scream my name."

Goddamn. He wanted that. "I'll give you anything."

Court's sexy chuckle rumbled through the air. "Damn right you will." He opened the door, letting light flood inside. As they stepped from the closet, two men halfway through changing looked their way. They stared as Court towed Heath toward the door. Heath smiled like an idiot. It was out of his control.

"Lucky motherfucker."

Heath's smile grew at the quietly spoken words mumbled behind them. Damn right. Heath had made all the mistakes and spent way too many years trying to please all the wrong people. He had been enslaved by his family and station. Now he owned the whole fucking world in just one person. He would never fail Court again. It was time for a happy life.

Keep an eye out for the next Atlantic City's Most Wanted, *Duped.*

Please consider leaving a review where you purchased this book. Every review counts and helps me continue to write. Thank you, Charity.

About the Author

CHARITY PARKERSON IS AN award-winning and multi-published author with several companies. Born with no filter from her brain to her mouth, she decided to take this odd quirk and insert it in her characters. One of her greatest loves is writing morally gray characters. You'll find them scattered throughout her hundreds of titles.

*Nine-time Readers' Favorite Award Winner

*2015 Passionate Plume Award Finalist

*2013 Reviewers' Choice Award Winner

*2012 ARRA Finalist for Favorite Paranormal Romance

*Five-time winner of The Mistress of the Darkpath

Connect with her online:

*Sign up for her newsletter: https://bit.ly/charityparkersonnewsletter

*Join her readers' group on Facebook: http://bit.ly/CharitysTribe

*Website: https://www.charityparkerson.com

*A list of her social media accounts and giveaways all in one place: http://hy.page/charityparkerson